# The Silly Book

*to Floosie*
*who is very silly*

# Babette Cole

# The Silly Book

RED FOX

If you look closely you'll agree,
there are some silly sights to see.

CUPIG

BOOPER
SCOOPER

Silly people passing by
have silly walks
that you can try!

Silly ears

and silly necks,

silly noses,

silly specs.

Silly beards

and silly teeth,

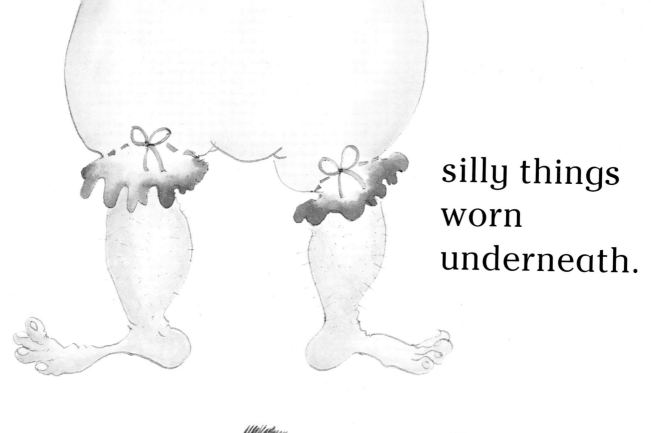

silly things
worn
underneath.

Silly hats are there to hide
some very silly heads inside!

And have you seen
how odd it gets

when silly folks
look like their pets?

Silly zebras,

silly bears,

# Some silly people like to fly,

I've never known
the reason why.

Babies eat some silly things,
like flies with wriggly legs and wings.

But grown-ups eat them just as well,
like wriggly frogs

and snails that smell.

My uncle Billy ate some fire.

His temperature went
higher and higher!

But auntie got the
teapot spout
and put poor
silly Billy out!

His friend, the Nabob of Namphilly,
had forty wives and all were silly.

They tickled him and not one stopped
until the poor old Nabob popped!

POP!

Don't play

silly party tricks

# With silly masks

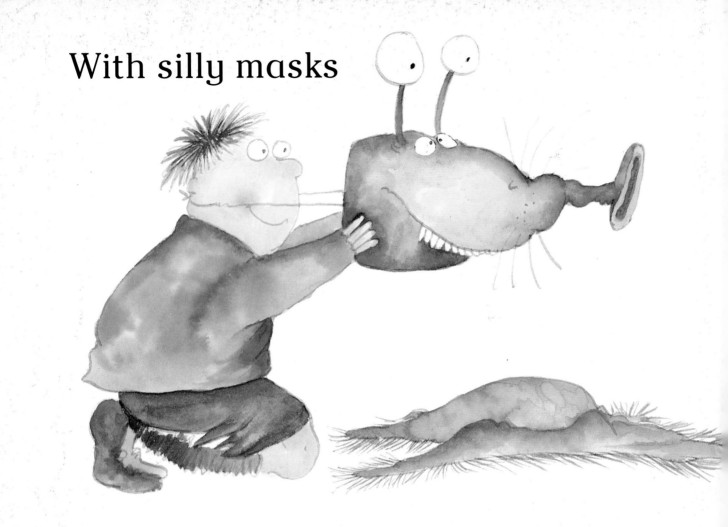

# and silly sheets,

for they can cause some silly SHRIEKS!

I hate being dressed in silly best,

with collar and
cuffs all frilly.

I'd rather wear my
plain wool suit . . .

It doesn't look
as silly!

A Red Fox Book

Published by Random House Children's Books
61-63 Uxbridge Road, London W5 5SA

A division of The Random House Group Ltd
London Melbourne Sydney Auckland
Johannesburg and agencies throughout the world

3 5 7 9 10 8 6 4

First published in Great Britain by Jonathan Cape Ltd, 1989
Published by Little Mammoth 1992

Red Fox edition 2001

Printed in Hong Kong by Midas Printing Ltd

THE RANDOM HOUSE GROUP Limited Reg. No. 954009

www.kidsatrandomhouse.co.uk

ISBN 0 09 941705 7

# More Red Fox picture books
# for you to enjoy

**ELMER**
by David McKee

**RUNAWAY TRAIN**
by Benedict Blathwayt

**DOGGER**
by Shirley Hughes

**WHERE THE WILD THINGS ARE**
by Maurice Sendak

**OLD BEAR**
by Jane Hissey

**MISTER MAGNOLIA**
by Quentin Blake

**ALFIE GETS IN FIRST**
by Shirley Hughes

**OI! GET OFF OUR TRAIN**
by John Burningham

**GORGEOUS**
by Caroline Castle and Sam Childs